united
p.c.

All rights of distribution, including via film, radio, and television, photo-mechanical reproduction, audio storage media, electronic data storage media, and the reprinting of portions of text, are reserved.

The author is responsible for the content and correction.

© 2016 united p. c. publisher

Printed in the European Union on environmentally friendly, chlorine- and acid-free paper.

www.united-pc.eu

Dream Crimes

Gabriela Naumnik

For Cysia

-NOTE FROM THE AUTHOR-

Whenever anybody asks me if "Janette", one of the stories you are about to read, belongs to fiction, I have a great difficulty with providing them with an accurate answer. On one hand, I dreamt both "Janette" and "Tiny House" up and then wrote them down to remember, so they are just a part of my peculiar imagination. On the other hand, certain fragments of my dreams turned into reality, which surprised me as well as scared a bit. Yet those were just those innocent parts of the stories you will explore. My best friend will know precisely which elements are true, which dates are real, and why I am referring to one character in terms of "Him". Each story, if considered fully, belongs to fiction, but this does not mean that those stories are one hundred percent imaginary to me. Both of them fascinated me, as they just came to me when I was peacefully sleeping in my bed, and I hope that you will engross yourself in "Janette" and "Tiny House" as much as I did.

-JANETTE-

12th May 2013

Janette kept staring at her Facebook timeline in futile search for companionship, yet nobody seemed to be a mind-reader willing to message her. She had checked the man's timeline for the *nth* time, but her friend request was not accepted. No wonder why. Janette was five years younger than Him and there was particularly little chance of Him paying any attention to her during those old days of primary school. But she, now almost twenty years old, kept thinking about Him. And those thoughts were nagging her, hellishly. Her dreams have always been very vivid, realistic and engrossing, each one constituting a great movie itself, yet there should be some limit to what we dream of.

Our mind is a mystery, which cannot be untangled in spite of our greatest willingness to find the reason for our subconsciousness's peculiar creations. I don't believe in magic, neither do I believe in any other form of spiritualism. But Janette's story made me wonder whether I should change my mind.

She saw Him for the first time at the age of eleven during the first day at the new school and fell in love with Him instantly. This was the kind of beautiful, youthful love for which the thought about the object of our interest is sufficient for feeling a bunch of happy butterflies in the stomach. And that was the case. Platonic, childish, pure love. He graduated after one year and Janette could see Him from time to time coming back to school to chat with the headmaster or visit some of the teachers. She hadn't talked to Him even once, but his face was one of a few, which she could see with her mind's eye in detail. She loved hearing him sing during each school's ceremony as much as she enjoyed watching Him perform as He was an extrovert, whom she imagined to become a popular actor one day. Having graduated from high school and having enrolled to one of the best middle schools in the country, Janette found a boyfriend and forgot about Him for a year.

Then the dream came.

They are in a black chamber with a ceiling which is so high that Janette can't see it. The walls are glistening and shaped like diamonds. All furniture is dark, some oriental ornaments may be viewed in spite of an overwhelming darkness. A black wardrobe is placed in the middle of the chamber; it's a huge wooden box on massive legs and it's the only piece of furniture with some white lines on it. They're running. Janette is scared. She doesn't know those elegantly dressed-in-black people. They want to protect her. Two of them open the wardrobe, somebody else lifts her and places her in the snowy-white inside of the wardrobe. They are shouting and telling her to stay there as "they are coming". Somebody else dressed in black jumps inside and barricades the door with a thick white wooden stick. They are alone inside of the wardrobe. Footsteps and shouts can be heard from the outside. Somebody is trying to open the wardrobe… Janette is scared… Then the man dressed in black turns to her and it's Him. She feels sick. He's wearing priest's overalls. He's looking at her in a way a stranger looks at another stranger and says something, but she cannot hear his words. She doesn't reply, she just keeps staring, hesitates for a moment, thinking, "He's a priest, but…", and she kisses Him. He pushes her away rapturously and brutally. He throws away the stick and quickly gets out of the wardrobe without even looking at her. She's left in the abyss of loneliness, and almost crying.

Suddenly, Janette is in a glorious hall. By contrast, it's white, yet the ceiling seems to be black. There are many people inside, all dressed in white and He's sitting with them. There's only one unoccupied chair in the room – next to Him. She takes a seat, she's sobbing. She looks at Him with no remorse, she cannot comprehend why he rejected her. He ignores her talking, yet casts a furtive glance at her face from time to time… She feels lost, she's crying even louder and louder…

A crowd gathers around her and Him. It's the end of a play. Suddenly, she can see an audience applauding behind her. She didn't know this wasn't real life! She's completely taken aback… He takes His gown off. Underneath, He's got regular clothes. He looks at Janette with joy in his eyes, says that "playing with her was a pleasure" and asks her out for a coffee. They leave the theatre together.

Janette woke up covered in cold sweat. That was weird. Why would she dream about Him? She has never dreamt about Him before; funny enough, she has never even dreamt about her own boyfriend. This dream was peculiar due to two reasons: first, it had the beginning, concrete action, and the ending; second, a guy she used to be smitten by suddenly became the key character of the dream. As it was Saturday morning, Janette took out a notebook and described the dream in detail adding a date of 12th May 2013. Something was making her feel uneasy about the dream though. She googled Him and kept staring at the result for a while. Yesterday it was added to His filmography that He played in one episode of a TV series, which Janette does not want me to name. There couldn't be any correlation between the dream and the addition of this piece of information, but Janette felt uncomfortable as it reminded her of the last year's events.

She had been dreaming of a white minivan for about a week. Those were short dreams, the minivan was just speeding into the darkness. Janette hadn't paid much attention to those silly visions till one Monday morning on her way to school. Her dad was driving and she was sitting in a passenger's seat. Suddenly a white minivan appeared speeding like crazy. Pedestrian crossing: no lights at all and an elderly woman carrying a lot of bags trying to reach the pavement on time. Too late. The minivan hit the woman with such an impact, that her fragile body was thrown a hundred metres away from the van. Her head was lying in a puddle of blood and the contents of the bags were scattered everywhere. The woman died on the spot.

16th February 2015

He walks with Janette through an elegant corridor and keeps telling her about a death in His family. Janette and He are close. He treats her as the only person to whom He may confess.

Janette woke up in cold sweat. The dream is back after two years. She fetched her MacBook and googled him immediately and got to know that he's recently starred in another movie. Janette thought about the first weird dream about Him being a priest and started googling more about him. Suddenly, she felt sick: there he was, dressed as a priest, sitting in an identical chamber she dreamed of and promoting His new play. Janette caught a glimpse of a date this video was posted – 17th December 2014, hence one year after her dream. This didn't feel normal. She left her room, walked downstairs and told her mum about those dreams. Her brother was eavesdropping and, eventually, started mocking her. They didn't understand anything. Well, that's not surprising. On one hand, coincidences do happen, but, on the other hand, they do not tend to be so specific. It was as if Janette's dreams were to predict the future. Yeah, this sounds just dumb and crazy. But, if it's dumb and crazy, there's solely one person who should understand it perfectly: Claire.

iMessage, 5:21 p.m.

Janette: Claire, I think I have some issues. With myself. And with those dreams.

Claire: What has happened?

Janette: This ain't normal.

Claire: :O

Janette: Do u remember when I told u about this dream about this guy and that I checked out his filmography and it showed that some info about him playing in a movie had been just uploaded? T'day it was exactly the case. I dreamt about him again and found out he's just finished filming another thing. I'm getting worried.

Claire: Shit.

Janette: Wtf, Claire? I'm normally not even thinking about the guy, but dream about him.

Claire: Maybe u read sth about him or somebody told u sth about him, and that's why your subconsciousness made u think about him.

Janette: No. Not at all.

Claire: U may not remember now.

Janette: I've made the whole analysis.

Claire: But ur subconsciousness does recall.

Janette: For sure NO

Claire: Maybe u two are... connected? :>

Janette: I haven't been thinking about this recently, u know. Fuck. This ain't normal. If this shit continues, I'll start seeing a psychologist.

Claire: hahahahahaha

Janette: Cause I'm getting scared.

Claire: They won't help u. Shrinks never help.

Janette: So how the fuck should I explain this?

Claire: I'll ask my friend :>

Janette: I'm uncomfortable with those dreams.

Claire: U have a gift maybe? hahaha xD

Janette: :(One more thing, Claire. U remember this dream about a priest?

Claire: Sure.

Janette: See the attachment.

Claire: What the fuck????!!! I really need to help u with this shit, Janette. My friend will surely get interested as well.

Janette: This clip was added on the 17th of December 2014. Wait I'll give u the date of the 1st dream...

Janette: 12th May 2013. Fuck. I don't like this. Or maybe I do? In a way, that's cool. He looked completely alike in my dream and so did the room.

Claire: As I said, u two are connected :>

Janette: No way. He doesn't even know I exist. T'day, in this dream, he was telling me about death in his family. That somebody's going to die.

Claire: If u dream about sth like that, it'd be wise to get in touch with him and, no matter how dumb this sounds, warn him.

Janette: Nooooo.

Claire: Well... I'm a realist, but I take everything with a grain of salt. I hope that there's a bit of magic in this world. Maybe we live in a movie? That's a good question.

Janette: Maybe?

Claire: Then u'll save his life, fall for him and he'll fall for u and u'll live happy ever after. Or u're gonna die.

Janette: Claire, hey, stop.

Claire: I'm just kidding.:> If it comes to the first possibility, the probability can be found in the set of real numbers, and the second is real as we aren't immortal yet.

Janette: Right. But the story is fantastic, right?

Claire: I'd make a great movie. Maybe u should even star in it? And him?! :D :D :D

Janette: I don't know the guy. Neither does he know me.

Claire: Who knows? Maybe he remembers u as u remember him? :>

Janette: No way. We were at the same school, but he was five years older, so he didn't pay any attention to me.

Claire: aha

Janette: He cannot possibly know me. We haven't even spoken once. But, as I know, this was the only guy I have been truly in love with.

Claire: Hahahah. That's sweet :)

Janette: Not sweat. Set. Sit. Sweet! Shit, the auto-correct.

Claire: I get it. I'll think about this.

Janette: The funny thing is that I haven't dreamt about any of my boyfriends. Like NEVER. U know what? I'm gonna go now and try to book a ticket for one of plays where he stars. Wanna come with me to any of those plays?

Claire: Sure thing. See u! No worries!

Janette went downstairs with the MacBook and saw her parents watching TV news. She sat next to her mum.

"Congressman Leon Bransky was found dead at his home an hour ago, police report. The cause of his demise was strangulation with a pillow. At the time of the tragedy, congressman's wife and four children were at the airport, on their way back home from a trip to Italy. At the moment, police are investigating. The murderer's identity remains unknown…"

Terrible stuff happens. Those are also the moments when you are so happy that your own family is here, safe and sound. Those are the moments, when you feel so grateful and so close to your loved ones. Janette put her head on her mother's shoulder. Then she booted the laptop and began the search for plays starring Him. There was only one play in a theatre, which was about 300 km away from Janette's hometown. Hmm... She's got two weeks of free time now due to the long weekend, so she could go there. Why not? She went upstairs, took her credit card, and booked two tickets for the play. Maybe Claire would like to come to keep her company. As Janette didn't have a driving licence (studying seemed more important at the moment), she purchased also a ticket for a bus. Claire should get her own ticket. Then, Janette called Claire.

"Hi! So, I booked two tickets for a play. See the attachment I sent you on Facebook."

"Wait... Right. Quite a long way, huh? I can do it though. I guess we'll go by bus?"

"Yes. You have to purchase the ticket yourself, I don't know your personal details."

"OK. I'll do it today. So we're going the day after tomorrow?"

"Yes! I'll tell my parents. This should be interesting."

"By the way, I've been doing some Tarot today. And I asked a question about your guy. I got the answer; that it would be better for you two not to meet."

"Why?"

"'Cause he's not a good person."

"We don't have to meet. We don't know each other. I just want to take a look at him. And I like creepy stuff, mysterious people and that kind of stuff."

"Here we go then! See you after tomorrow at the bus stop!"

"See you!"

18th February 2015

The play was about to start at 6.00 p.m. Janette and Claire arrived thirty minutes earlier to take a look around the theatre. There were some photos of Him hanging on the walls and Janette felt a bit silly about the whole venture. She didn't even really want to see this play as it was supposed to be a tragedy about a king, who had many homosexual partners – not a spectacle to create a relaxing mood. The first gong told the girls to take their seats and so they did. After the third gong, the room fell into darkness and the play began.

He was a great actor. Young, yet so spectacular. He's got a bright future awaiting Him, Janette thought. He made this terrible play fantastic. When the spectators started leaving, Claire looked at Janette with her questioning eyes. "So what do we do?"

"What do you mean?"

"We didn't come here just to watch the play, right? This was not your goal."

"I know. But what am I supposed to do, hmm? Go to his dressing room and say 'hi, I've been dreaming about you for the past couple of years and I'd like to warn you that something terrible may happen to you family'? Claire, that's just dumb."

"So why did you drag me all the way down here?"

"Didn't you like the play and time with me?"

"I did enjoy it, but now, I do feel rather disappointed."

"Claire…"

"Listen. We are weird people. You have those dreams and I like risk. I love taking risks and this is one of the reasons why I walk in the forest at night. I'm crazy. So, the plan is the following: I'm gonna go and use my connections to make him interested in going out with us for a drink, OK?"

"Whatever. What connections do you have?"

"Do you know Tony Sparks?"

"Yes, he's a legendary actor and one of the most famous filmmakers."

"Indeed. I met him once and have his business card. I'll make this actor of yours believe Tony Sparks is my uncle."

"Holy shit. I see your point now."

"Let's go."

Claire dragged Janette towards the actors' dressing rooms and managed to bump straight into Him. At the same time, Janette was sitting a few metres away from them.

"Hi!" Claire grinned at Him.

"Good evening." He looked a bit startled.

"I'm Tony Spark's niece and have an offer for you coming from him." Claire looked at Him in a serious way.

"Wow, that's unexpected. What is this offer about?"

"A movie. He'd like you to play in 'Dragon's Five' and sent me to ask you if, first, you're interested; second, if yes, ordered me to interview you to check if you're well suited for this movie. Is this all right with you?"

"Yes. Should we grab a drink and discuss the details?"

"Certainly. I'm here with a friend, so hope you don't mind."

"Not at all. Where is she?"

Claire pointed at Janette, who was tapping on her iPhone.

"Janette, come over here!" Claire waved at her friend.

"Coming!" Janette put her phone back in her purse and approached Claire and Him.

"Hi, I'm Janette." She reached her hand towards Him and they shook hands. Janette always stuck to the rule that a handshake should be strong. When you grab somebody's hand you need to show them that you're confident. Nobody wants to shake hands with somebody whose hand is like a sponge. Another rule is to smell nice. This may seem insignificant, but good-quality perfumes make others remember you. Janette learned this at school. Sometimes she was not wearing perfumes and then she smelled of nothing. But, when she used just a drop of them, some of her peers tended to compliment her on the smell and asked for the brand. Claire made her realise this. She would know exactly when Janette was perfumed and when she was not. Janette also realised that men were more likely to hit on her when she was wearing just a few drops of her favourite smell.

"Hi, I'm..." He scrutinised Janette with His piercing eyes.
"We're going to grab something to drink together and discuss his role in my uncle's movie as I told you."
Claire looked at Janette.

"Of course, let's go."

"I'll drive us," he offered enthusiastically.
When they were heading towards the garage, Janette looked in utter fury at Claire and whispered,

"What the hell? What kind of movie? Don't you think that's too much to say?"

"This is actually true. Tony Sparks will be making a movie entitled 'Dragon's Five'. I googled this yesterday. So, we're going to pretend our actor friend has a chance of getting a part. As I know castings are ongoing, so he'll deal with it by himself. Maybe he'll get a part. And, in the meantime, you should try to make him feel smitten by you. If you'd like. We have nothing to lose and may have some fun."

"You're crazy. I don't know whether I should love you or hate you."

"I love you, you know that."

They parked the car near the pub and headed inside. The place was completely crowded, but they managed to find a free table and ordered one beer and two mojitos. Jenny was sitting next to Claire and He was sitting opposite them. Jenny glanced at Claire confidently and began the conversation.

"Tell us first, how do you feel about this proposal?"

"I'm quite shocked, frankly speaking. I'm also honoured that somebody as well known as Tony Sparks is willing to offer me a part." He sighed.

"Fantastic. There's a strong probability you'll be chosen to play a lonely man, who lost some of his family members in an accident. You will have to be realistic here. Your sorrow will have to be genuine to the viewer. Can you relate any of this to your personal experience?" Claire asked.

"I haven't lost anybody yet, but I can assure you that I will do my best to get into this character."

"OK. There's my uncle's business card. Call him. He tends to forget many things, 'cause he's particularly busy, but, if you make a good impression, you should get this part. There are hundreds of candidates, you know. And new ones are joining the group of those willing to get the part each day." Claire took a serious tone.

Janette looked magnificent. She was wearing a black, tight-fitting dress. Her pale skin and long, black hair as well as red lips and big, dark eyes made her look as if she was a painted figure. Her white teeth and sincere smile made Him feel a bit overwhelmed. She was stunning. Her friend, Claire was also a beautiful woman. Her ginger hair and green eyes made her particularly original, yet there was something about Janette He couldn't explain. Maybe it was her eyes, glancing at Him in such a peculiar manner. He didn't know. Yet, He was sure He'd like to spend more time with them to get to know a bit more about these angels of good news and opportunity.

"We'll be back in a second," Janette informed Him and took Claire with her to the bathroom.

"Don't tell me that his character will have to be a lonely man, you were just playing."

"I was. Who cares? I might have confused the roles. I might forget easily." She grinned. "He'll talk to Tony Sparks and be happy with that. Maybe he'll even manage to get a part? But look, now we know that his family is safe and sound. So the question is: for how long?"

"You seem really into my dreams, huh? Let's go back home, Claire. There's no point in digging deeper. Dreams will remain dreams."

"Don't you want to get to know him?" Claire blinked.

"I'm not particularly emotional and you know that. The guy is freaking handsome and I've been dreaming about being his girlfriend at primary school, but I'm a grown-up now and see no point in getting into a relationship with a man I don't know."

"He likes you."

"Sure he does. I smile, smell nice, have long hair and red lips and dudes are shitting their pants. I got used to this. This is his problem."

"I'm hungry."

"Really?" Janette sighed. "Eat as much as you want, but I'm not talking to this charming guy."

After having this conversation, the girls spent two more hours with Him, chatting and laughing. He turned out to be quick-witted and a talented story-teller. Eventually, they (being a bit drunk) exchanged phone numbers and parted.

19th February 2015

He called Janette in the evening to ask her out. She and Claire could stay in the city for a few days more, so Janette agreed to meet Him in the park and decided to take Claire with her. The girls dressed casually and headed for the meeting.

They met in a cosy cafe near the park and, after one hour, Claire told Him and Janette that she had to go due to an important conversation she was supposed to have on Skype. Janette was left alone with Him.

They realised they shared common passions such as detective stories and French language. Janette also realised that He didn't remember her at all from school. She didn't tell Him about this, but conducted the conversation in such a manner, that He eventually was taken aback by the fact that they must have been at the same school. Common experience brought them closer as they could discuss their old teachers and their foibles as well as the headmaster's crazy ideas. They laughed a lot and, close to midnight, He walked Janette back to the apartment she rented for a couple of days with Claire.

20th February 2015 - 22nd November 2015
Janette and Him kept on seeing each other for a couple of months during which they became close friends. There weren't a couple, they hadn't even kissed once. They were just great buddies, spending hours on long conversations touching upon big ideas for movies and books. Their creativity was impressive and they even decided to write a script together. Claire wasn't willing to participate in the process as she found a new boyfriend to whom she was sacrificing the majority of her time. Everything

seemed perfect till the day of the 22nd of November when another dream came:

Janette was talking on the phone with Him. She didn't know whether He called her or she called Him. They'd been talking for a long time, Janette was mostly speaking and He didn't say much. The feeling of sadness and emptiness came all over her. It was as if He was pushing her away, yet couldn't let her go. He wanted to listen to her sad voice. They'd been talking twice on the phone and the connection broke down once. Janette didn't know what they were talking about, but this was a conversation filled with sadness and despair.

Janette woke up and dwelled on the dream. She fetched her notebook and wrote everything down. Should she call Him? He's a close friend of hers now. What should she tell Him? This is ridiculous. Janette started analysing past dreams. In the first dream, He was playing a priest and was pushing her away in the play, but in reality was her buddy. This proved to be true. He played a priest and became her second best friend (Claire was her first best friend). In the second dream, He was confessing to her about death in His family. This dream had obviously nothing to do with reality as there was no premature death in His family. He claimed this to be true Himself. In the third dream, they were talking about something unpleasant on the phone and He wanted to let her go, yet couldn't. The first dream became reality after approximately one year. It's December now. Should this signify that in 2016, somebody from His family will die and their friendship will hang on a thread? That's possible, but also entirely stupid.

1st December 2015

Janette met Him on the 1st December, one day after His return from shooting scenes for "Dragon's Five" in Spain (he managed to get a supporting role, but remained a bit pissed off due to the fact that Tony Sparks didn't "remember" him). He was nicely sunbathed, which looked fantastic with His blond hair and blue eyes. He became more muscular and Janette thought that she liked His appearance. There is no real friendship between a man and a woman and Janette knew this well. At least from the man's side. She used to go out with men, whom she treated solely in a friendly manner, but, sadly, had to realise each time that from their point of view they were "dating". This is why many of her "friendships" with men ended. If it came to Him, she was not sure what His point of view on their relationship was, yet she enjoyed treating Him like a friend and was not willing to be romantic. She didn't have time for that and had been let down way too many times.

They went to His apartment, made some coffee, logged on to His laptop and started revising their ideas for a movie script. They'd been working for an hour and got really hungry, so He went to purchase some food from a Japanese restaurant nearby. Janette was left alone.

She looked around the room and realised that His actor's pay had to be quite large. He possessed many expensive accessories and electronics. Suddenly, Janette realised that the laptop needed to be recharged immediately, thus she started to look for a charger. She couldn't find it anywhere nearby, so she went to His bedroom and started searching His desk. No charger. Where the hell was the charger?! She glanced at the inside of a tiny drawer containing scattered photos. So He likes photography, she thought. There were many pics showing city streets, flowers, His fellow actors, the theatre and… Holy shit.. Janette took a photo out of the drawer and couldn't take her eyes off it. There were three people in the picture. A woman was sitting with a child on a bed and a man was hugging them. There was a signature on the backside of the photo saying "you, your mother and your father". This was a beautiful picture showing the atmosphere of a loving home. Yet, something was all wrong about it. And what was wrong about it was the fact that the man on the photo was Leon Bransky – the strangled congressman Janette heard about on the news on the 16th of February 2015. Of course, this could be His father, but why did He lie then about a death in His family? They asked Him about prematurely deceased family members barely a few days after the strangulation. He lied to them. And His father was strangled for goodness sake! This is not a usual situation! They will have to have a serious talk tonight. She put the photo back in place and headed towards the living room where she had to wait for ten more minutes for His arrival with food.

"I'm back!" She heard Him taking off His shoes and locking the door.

"Great." Her voice sounded harsh.

He entered the living room and stared at her in surprise.

"Something's wrong, Janette?" He looked concerned.

"Yes. I'll be honest with you. Just sit down." He sat down and put the packed food aside. "I've been looking for the charger. I couldn't find it here, so I decided to see if it was in your desk. Then I found the drawer with photos and saw the picture with Leon Bransky, who's supposed to be your father. Wait. Let me finish before you say anything. I'm sorry for searching your stuff. I'm sorry. But, that is not about me looking for your charger now. The thing is that you lied to us, me and Claire, when we asked you about death in the family. You said everything was fine and your father had been then dead for a few days due to strangulation. Why did you lie?"

He sat with His mouth wide open for a few seconds, then sighed and said slowly, "Because I didn't want to discuss such matters with you then. You were two girls I had never met before and I reckoned that discussing a murder in my family wouldn't be a wise approach. This hurts me, this is an uncomfortable topic for me. I'd like to forget about the whole thing."

"I'm sorry for your loss. I've just always been honest with you, I've been confiding in you. You now know some stuff about me nobody else knows. That's why I assumed you've been honest with me all the time. I'm not angry. I'm sorry this happened to you."

"Thank you." He swallowed hard.

"Do you know who killed your father?"

"No, I don't." He shook His head and started staring at His feet.

"You were close with your dad?" Janette stared at Him with compassion.

"No. I haven't seen my father for years now. When I was a kid, he sent me to this school you attended as well and I was living in a dorm. I've spent the majority of my life in dorms. I've never had a real home. I decided never to treat my father as a real one, 'cause he's never been a father to me."

"What about your mother? She didn't care about you either?"

"She died when I was one year old, so I didn't really know her."

"I'm sorry. What happened?"

"Janette, this conversation hurts me…" His eyes suddenly became wet.

"End of the conversation then. Come here." He sat next to her and Janette started holding Him in her arms. "I will never return to this conversation again. I promise." She gazed into those blue eyes of His and smiled gently. "Never ever ever again."

2nd December 2015

They woke up at 2.00 a.m. on His couch with empty stomachs, so they ate cold takeaway in silence. This was a bit awkward as they slept on the same couch and thoughts about the conversation made Janette feel uneasy. She felt sorry for His unhappy childhood and so much tragedy in the family. She had so many questions, but dared not ask. She wanted to know His mother's name. Instead, she said, "I have an idea for the script."

"What is that?" He seemed relaxed.

"I'd call it 'The story of two bins'. One lawyer told me this story at a wedding. There was a married couple living in a block of flats. This was the kind of block of flats, where each apartment in a column is identical. The man had an affair with a woman living exactly above his apartment. One night, he sneaked out of his home and went to his lover living upstairs. She asked him to do her a favour and take the garbage out. So he went outdoors and fulfilled her request. Subsequently, he went upstairs with an empty bin in hand and entered the apartment. Having entered the kitchen and having opened the cupboard, he realised there had already been a bin placed on the floor. That was the moment he realised he had entered his home, not his lover's. That was also the instant his wife turned the lights on and became sure of his treachery. She filed for divorce and they don't keep in touch. And that, my dear, is a real story. What do you say?"

"It's a great story, Janette. We could develop it and write a reasonable script."

"Perfect. This food you brought is delicious by the way. Even if it's cold."

"Heheh. Good. Don't you have to go back home? You don't have a free day tomorrow."

"I have to. Can you drive me?"

"Sure I can."

He dropped her on the driveway, but before leaving, He informed Janette that, in two days, He was going abroad for a week to shoot for a movie. She wished Him a lucky journey and went home to analyse the whole situation. He wasn't honest with her, but why would he be? They had known each other for a few months and she hadn't told him many things either. But he didn't ask for them and this made the whole difference. If you're not asked about something, you have no reason to share what you know with another person. Your life belongs to you and privacy is precious. Eventually, Janette grabbed her phone and called Claire to tell her the recent news. Her friend was furious due to such an early call, but listened carefully.

"I'm sorry for him. That's terrible. What happened to his mother?"

"No clue. I promised him never to bring this topic back."

"Should we find out?"

"How and why are you willing to find this out?"

"My aunt is a lawyer."

"My dad is a doctor."

"Why are you bringing your dad into this?"

"And why are you bringing your auntie?"

"You're teasing me, right? My aunt has connections and could find out something about this death."

"OK. My dad could search for some info about the causes of death. Because...something must have happened to her, right? From the photo I know that she was younger than Leon Bransky, so...Jesus..."

"This becomes creepy. You shouldn't panic though. She could have been seriously ill or something."

"That's highly probable. Talk to your aunt, I'll discuss this with my dad. I, personally, am not able to do much here."

"They should help us. She must have died 24 years ago if that was one year after his birth."

"That's a lot of time…"

"Wait, let's not bring our relatives into this. We should just go to the registry office and find out what is written in the death certificate."

"We don't know her name, but she died twenty-four years ago and her surname must have been…"

"Possibly not Bransky, because our actor friend is not named Bransky."

"He couldn't have changed his surname, because at school he had the same surname as today."

"Right. So this is helpful. We should look for a woman deceased twenty-four years ago at the age of around twenty, who had the same surname as her son."

"So far so good. Claire, should we assume she and the congressman were not married?"

"I think so. In case of marriage, the child takes on his or her father's surname."

"Is Leon married now? I mean, was he?"

"I'll google that…"

"And?"

"He was married and has four kids."

"That's a lot of kids."

"Meet me tomorrow at 5.00 p.m. in front of the registry. Sweet dreams."

"G'night." Janette hung up and closed her eyes. She didn't sleep well that night.

3rd December 2015

So she was epileptic. Janette shook her head and took a sip of coffee. They were sitting with Claire at the latter's place and discussing their recent trip to the registry office.

"No wonder he didn't feel like discussing his family situation. That's a bad situation and when I say 'bad', I really mean it." Claire put her mug down and stood up. She started pacing up and down the room and eventually turned on her laptop, googled "Bransky" and began reading out loud. "'...The cause of Bransky's death was strangulation with a pillow. The murderer remains unknown, but it is widely believed that the oppressor's motive was linked to the congressman's political activity...' What do you think, Janette?"

Janette sighed. "I don't know. We don't know and won't know. I've never talked to this guy."

"You said the same about your other friend, my dear."

"I know, but... Claire, this whole case is shitty and the only reason why I care is because Leon was his father. But I won't care anymore. And I don't care about this politician, because I've never liked his activity either. He did more harm than good to our economy and was entirely delusional. You cannot lower taxes, decrease the retirement age, and spend more than ever before if the country is in debt. He was irrational and didn't listen to the youngest part of the population. What's more, he was corrupt. You know this well and agree with me."

"I agree with you, Janette, but I've always been curious. Don't you really want to bring up this topic with him again?"

"I don't and I won't." Janette stood up and went to the bathroom.

Claire kept on shouting from the other room. "Think about it! She died while having an attack of epilepsy! She hit herself on the head and this injury led to immediate death!"

"Shit happens! Stop shouting at me!" Janette flushed the toilet and returned to the room where Claire was sitting. "Stop digging into this, Claire. There's no damn point. This man deserved to die. He sucked at his job and cared nothing about his son."

"You're evil to say that. As you said, we know nothing. Maybe he was a great father to the rest of his kids? Don't judge him. Your actor friend may have not told you the whole truth, you know. Who cares?"

"I'll try to talk to him. I now see that he has no one close in here and saying out loud stuff, which has been bothering you for ages may be a genuine blessing. I have to go now."

16th December 2015

Janette had spent the last couple of hours working with Him on the script. They got on well, maybe too well. He told Janette an overheard story about a woman who was driving a car at night and suddenly realised she had been followed. She parked at the petrol station, filled the tank and went to pay the bill. When she returned, her follower's car was parked nearby and a man was sitting inside. She approached his car, opened his door and furiously yelled at him for following her. His answer was calm and simple. "I wanted to warn you. You were driving with a man sitting at the back. When you parked and went to pay I saw him leaving your car. He saw me and that's why he left. I knew he was there." The story was particularly terrifying as it was true. They decided to fit it somehow into their script.

"Listen," Janette said gently, "you can tell me what happened in your family. I can't leave you like that. And this knowledge about your past makes me uncomfortable. I can't pretend I feel fantastic."

"Can I trust you?"

"Sure you can trust me."

"I want to ask you about something first before I tell you my story. Do you have feelings for me?"

Janette hesitated. She had never had genuine feelings for a man. In this case, however, she wasn't sure. She had cared about Him for the majority of her life. He has been her first love, then the hero of her visions. And now, there he was, sharing so much with her. She knew she wouldn't be able to give him up and not care about His wellbeing and happiness. He was also the only person in the world she shared her passion with.

"I care about you a lot in a way I've never cared about anyone else. I've never been in love, if that's what you're asking for, but I do have feelings for you." Janette looked serious.

"I will tell you the story then. I don't remember my mother as I told you. She died when I was only one year old, so there's no way I could remember her. My father has never been taking care of me. I've spent the majority of my life with a nurse. My parents could afford for her to live with me wherever I was as my mother originated from an opulent German family. My father promised to marry her, but this didn't happen due to her premature death. She was epileptic. One day, she had the attack in a tiny bathroom and hit the toilet with such an impact that there was no chance of bringing her back to life. The whole loo was covered in blood, her brains sunk into the carpet. Horrible. Before dying, she made an official will that all of her assets be given to my father in case of death. My father didn't have much before meeting my mother, but her death made him a wealthy man. This is also how he managed to pursue a political career. He sucked at economics, he sucked at everything. But he was malicious. My mother didn't die by accident. My father, Leon Bransky, killed her. She had the attack in the bathroom, this is true. When my fucking father heard the noise and saw what was going on, he took her head and threw it with incredible force on the toilet. My mother's head was in pieces. He murdered her to get money. Money! He would have had access to it anyways! He was a fucking bastard. Interestingly, my nurse was at home at this moment and knew well the truth. She was too terrified though and never said anything to anybody about the murder. This job paid well and she was the only supplier for her family. She had a hard life, you know. When my father became wealthy, he made me live in my nurse's home. He didn't give a shit about me. He married a model after one year and had a happy life. Depending on what your definition of happiness is. He was sending me money and kept on financing my education. I stopped giving a shit about him. I even used to think that he loved me — that was ridiculous, but this was what the nurse was telling me. Kids always see the world through a pink prism. I began taking care of myself at the age of sixteen, when I no longer had to live with an adult. This was also the time my nanny wanted to have a serious talk with me. We met at my dorm in the evening, she took out the old photo you found in my drawer and told me the whole truth. She claimed that the only reason this photo was taken was to make us look like a happy family, so to eliminate any suspicion. And this photo was taken one day before my mother's murder. I reckoned that my father's plan went perfectly well until my conversation with the nurse. I promised to myself that I would never let him sleep peacefully. I called him and told him what I knew. I threatened to go to the police. I said I had a witness. I said that if something happened to my nanny, I'd incriminate him, that everybody would know. That I would ruin his fucking reputation. He got scared, because he loved his shitty life. He was supposedly a happy murderer. And you know what? I will tell you everything as I trust you, or maybe I no longer give a damn." He looked Janette deep in the eyes; she suddenly felt sick. "One night, the nurse called me and said my father started threatening her. She added that somebody'd been searching her house. I met my father on the 16th February to talk this over. I came by car so that my shoes were clean. My father's house has heated pavements, so there is never snow on them. My shoes were clean. I was wearing gloves. When I entered the house, somebody started strangling me with a pillow – my damn father! I had to defend myself and strangled him with the very same pillow. There was a moment when I considered keeping him alive, but couldn't see any reason why this should happen. He was a dirty bastard. He killed my mother, made my life miserable, threatened the only good woman I knew in my childhood and was a shitty politician. He deserved to die. I left the place without leaving a trace. This is the story you wanted to hear. What will you do about it now?" His facial expression became tense as he clenched his fists. Janette hesitated for a moment. He wasn't "not a good person" as Claire said once. Her first dream became reality. Her second dream became reality and so did her third dream as they had important, though saddening conversations. And they had exactly two such conversations, just like in the dream.

"I will keep this to myself," Janette said quietly. "Sometimes the truth is way too complicated to reveal it to others."

Suddenly, Janette's phone rang. It was Claire. Janette looked Him in the eyes and picked up.

"Hello?"

"Janette, my cards weren't lying. Get the hell out of there. Smile at him and just leave." She hung up.

This was also the instant Janette felt as lost and as overwhelmed as in all of her three dreams.

-THE END-

-TINY HOUSE-
2nd February 2015

Edward Thompson, a freelance journalist in his forties, was sitting in his living room and scrutinising a wedding invitation he had just received. Finally, his sister was about to get married to his old buddy, James Frank. Fantastic! He had always been wondering why they were waiting so long, as the couple kept on dating for about ten years. And eventually, the good news came. Edward was simply exhilarated, yet saddened due to the distance he would have to travel to attend the ceremony – more than 600 km. The obstacle was that there were neither any direct trains available from his hometown to the place where his sister had been living for the past five years with James, nor any flights. So, willy-nilly, Edward would have to go there by car. What about accommodation? Where should he sleep for those couple of days? He would have to figure this out, but he was almost late for a meeting with Jonathan Kozinsky, a well-established poetry writer. He put the invitation into a pocket of his thick brown coat (winter was particularly severe this year), which looked dashing along with his chocolate complexion and light hair, and headed towards a bar where they kept on meeting as often as possible. When he walked in, Jonathan had already been sitting at a table with a newspaper. Edward took off his coat and approached his buddy with a wide grin.

"Jonathan! How are you, man?"

Jonathan stood up and they shook hands.

"Ed, it's great to see you!" He squinted his eyes. "I have a gut feeling something must have happened, huh? Why are you showing me all of those gorgeous white teeth of yours?"

"My sis is getting married!" Edward looked amazingly happy.

"Congrats! That's fantastic! They should have made up their minds a couple of years ago though, haha. I'm happy for you."

"They should have, right? They have been living together for the last six years, they even bought a dog, whom they named Hamlet (better not ask…)" Edward laughed.

"When is the wedding?" Jonathan took two menus from a waitress who walked past their table.

"17th of February, take a look at the invitation." He showed Jonathan the elegant card. "So quite soon. I will book a hotel room when I come back home."

"Are you taking your wife with you?"

"Sally? I wish I could, but she is in Shanghai now on a delegation and is returning in May, so nope." Edward sighed.

"Well, this gives you a nice opportunity to make new acquaintances…" Jonathan blinked and Edward smiled wickedly at him.

"You will never change, Jon. I love you for that, man. By the way…"

"Wait!" Jonathan smiled. "I'll let you finish, but I've just recalled something. Show me the address again." Edward handed him the invitation, Jonathan smiled.

"Perfect, you don't need to pay for a hotel. An old friend of mine has a tiny house in this town. She doesn't really use it, but lets me go there from time to time to write my poetry and contemplate. The house is very small, but cosy and quiet. I can let my friend know that you're coming and give you the keys tomorrow or even fetch them for you tonight. What would you say, Eddie?"

"That would facilitate a lot and I could make some savings. Are you sure this wouldn't be an issue?"

"Not at all. Believe me, I know her well."

"Thank you, Jonathan." Edward smiled. "You always know how to make my life easier and myself richer." They laughed.

The men left the bar after one hour and drove to Jonathan's apartment to watch a game. Edward left after two hours with keys, happy and looking forward to the wedding party. Before going to bed, he also called his wife to describe to her the day's events and tell her how much he loved her as he tended to do rather often. And, of course, to get a piece of advice about what kind of a wedding gift to purchase. What would he do without her?

16th February 2015

The wedding was about to take place tomorrow at 1.00 p.m., so Edward decided to reach his destination earlier. As his wife advised him, he did not buy anything typical for the newly-weds. He decided to give his younger sister something special – a set of five paintings made by their great-grandmother. They were particularly beautiful and would certainly suit their house. Moreover, his sister should be surprised as she had never known that he actually possessed those works of art. Maybe he was hiding them as he was afraid his sister would start begging him to give them to her? She had always been an avid painter and became an art critic, so there was no doubt she was going to appreciate such a gift.

Edward reached his destination at midnight and was thoroughly exhausted. The house was named accurately as it was tiny indeed and looked like a classic house, which a three-year-old kid would draw: a square with a window and entrance on the ground floor and the first floor looking like a triangle with another window and a chimney sticking out of the roof. Oh, there was also a garage attached. There was no fence, but a lot of snow which was increasing in volume as it was snowing constantly in this part of the country in February. There was a road on the left side on the house, and a duplex on the right side. Edward opened the garage and parked inside. He was barely able to stand due to sleepiness, so he took his suitcase upstairs and fell asleep immediately.

17th February 2015

"Who is this man?!" Edward heard the scream of a young woman leaning over him. He glanced at his watch: it was 2.00 a.m. She started shaking him by the shoulders. "Wake up! Wake up! Can you hear me?!" She sounded furious.

"Leo! Do something!" She looked at a dark-haired man in utter fury.

So a man called "Leo" approached Edward, who felt completely paralysed by fear.

"Who are you?" Leo was scrutinising Edward, who could not utter a single word. He cleared his throat.

"I'm Edward. Calm down. Jonathan was supposed to tell you," he looked at a blond woman, "that I was about to spend a couple of days here. My sister is getting married tomorrow."

The couple looked totally taken aback. They stared at each other. Eventually, the woman said, "Oh, I must have forgotten. But my husband and I are going to sleep in here today, so you need to sleep downstairs."

"But not on the couch," Leo looked at his wife, "Because… it's broken, right, honey?"

"Yes."

Edward now felt furious. "But there is only one twin-bed here and downstairs, apart from kitchen, there are two armchairs and a couch. Do you want me to sleep on the floor?" Edward felt ridiculous and simultaneously angry as Jonathan must have forgotten to inform the owner about his visit.

"You need to sleep in the backseat of your car then," Leo said in a firm voice.

Now, Edward felt simply humiliated. Great, he thought. He drove all his way down here to sleep in that bloody car! He would speak to Jonathan tomorrow. How could he possibly be in good shape during the ceremony? "All right." Edward sighed and stood up slowly.
Leo took his suitcase. "I will help you."

The garage was heated, so Edward did not need to wear his coat. Before leaving, Leo put Ed's suitcase on the floor. "We're extremely sorry for this situation, man. Wait a second." He fetched a pillow and a blanket, which were lying on the armchairs. "Hope this helps." Leo handed them to Edward. The latter jumped.

"Ouch!" He started rubbing his shoulder. It hurt.

"I need to change my watch, it scratches every-thing. Sorry. And goodnight." Leo showed a faint smile and closed the door. Edward had an impression of a key rasping in the door, but he was too tired to take any notice.

Ed woke up at 12.00 p.m. and headed towards a kitchen. The woman had already been there, surrounded by tapes and plastic bags. She leaped when she heard Edward enter the kitchen. "Oh! You're up!"

"Yes I am. Wow!" He glanced at a clock. "It's 12.00 p.m.?!" He could not imagine how it was possible for him to sleep this long. "Listen, I feel stupid about the whole situation."

"We just messed up the dates. You know, we're a young couple, crazy and in love, haha." She laughed.

"I will move out as quickly as possible and leave you two alone."

"We're leaving today, so feel free to stay. I messed up the dates for which I too am sorry." She looked sorry. "What was your name?"

"Edward. And yours?"

"Olga."

"Nice to meet you, Olga. And Leo is your husband, right?"

"No, he's my boyfriend." She smiled again and so did Edward. He was pretty sure she had referred to him as her "husband". But he was tired then, so forget that.

"And what are you doing with all of those tapes and bags?"

"I'm cleaning up. I need to sort some things out... You know. When you're at home, there's a lot of stuff to do and rearrange. Would you like some coffee?"

He thankfully accepted. Suddenly, Leo entered the kitchen. "Good morning, honey! Good morning... what was your name?"

"Edward." They shook hands.

"I'm really sorry for this situation, man."

"Well, I remember that when I was this young and in love, and tended to forget many things..." He smiled. He was actually quite able to comprehend the situation, yet could not manage to feel comfortable.

"We're leaving today, Edward," Leo said, "so you can stay as long as you want. And now you have our word, we won't be coming back."

18th February 2015

The wedding was splendid. Edward's sister looked magnificent and he had never seen her as happy as on the 17th of February 2015. He would not be even able to put his feelings into words as that wedding day filled him with so many positive emotions. He felt grateful for his sister's good fortune. The wedding day and the party were simply perfect, or maybe almost. The witness, Harry Bellman, did not show up. He was supposed to come earlier, yet there was no trace of him anywhere. He was well-known for his time-management issues, but this was why he was told to come much earlier. Yet, he had never appeared at the wedding. Many people called him; even Edward was trying to reach the witness even though he had seen him barely once in his lifetime and never really managed to talk to him. The search turned out to be futile. Harry Bellman was single and an orphan, so there was nobody with whom they could get in touch to understand what happened to Harry. Even Uncle Frank, the witness' closest friend, had no clue about what had prompted such a lack of responsibility. Everybody decided to wait one more day and then, contact the police.

When Edward returned to the Tiny House, his phone rang. It was Justin, one of his wealthiest cousins, whom he happened to bump into at the wedding.

"Eddie, a good friend of mine invited me for a dinner tonight. I met him a week ago and he seems to be a really cool chap. He owns a restaurant called the Eagle and I got an invitation for tonight at 9.00 p.m. It was written that I could bring somebody, so I thought of you! What would you say? Do you have time?"

"And who's this friend of yours?"

"Dane Donton. You're gonna love him. He's a gifted story teller. Bizarre sometimes, but, as a journalist, you could certainly find some interesting topics to discuss with him."

"Seems alright. You said 9.00 p.m. tonight?"

"Yes. Let's meet at the Eagle, OK? I'll be waiting near the entrance."

"See you then. And thanks for inviting me."

"Love you, Eddie." Justin hung up.

Edward took his phone and googled the restaurant, which turned out to be rather far away from the Tiny House. Something was telling him it would be better to stay at the Tiny House and sleep, and this thought reminded him of a need to call Jonathan.

"Hi, buddy! How was the wedding?" Jonathan sounded as enthusiastic and as lively as usual.

"Jon, you forgot to inform the owner about me coming to stay. Man… I had a really embarrassing situation after arrival. This friend of yours came with a boyfriend and they were about to get into bed, when they spotted me, the lady started shouting, and, eventually, I had to sleep in the garage. I have never been put in such a situation, Jon."

"Ed, I spoke to the owner. She said that this was no problem; that you could stay. I gave her all the details and she told me that she did not have any plans to visit that place in the next couple of weeks." Jonathan sounded rather taken aback.

"So she must have forgotten, and brought a man along with her. I even can bet they locked me in the garage to be sure that I wouldn't disturb them."

"Oh! Wow! So she has a man! That's news! There she goes! She did not tell me, weird. Or maybe not, we haven't had much time to catch up recently."

"Anyways, it's 8.00 a.m. now (the party was out of this world!) and I need to rest, 'cause Justin invited me to a dinner organised by some kind of Dane Donton."

"Have fun then. I have a flight to Athens in two hours, so I'll call you when I get back." He hung up and Edward sighed. He did not feel like going to this dinner.

The Eagle was located 40 km from the city in the middle of a forest. It was dark, yet the view was undoubtedly something. The restaurant was combined with a hotel and looked marvelous in the moonlight. The beams of the ground lights emphasised the whiteness and elegance of the building, whose southern part was faced by a lake. Edward contemplated the view while parking his car, then headed towards the entrance, where Justin was awaiting him.

"It's great to see you, Edward." Justin stretched his hand towards Edward, they shook hands. "Let's go inside and meet the host."

They entered the building and Edward realised how expensive-looking the interior was. Walls were covered in scarlet as well as dark green wallpaper, which resembled silk. (Or maybe that was genuine silk?) There were many portraits hanging from the walls and each of them was in a golden frame. (Was that real gold?) Each piece of furniture was possibly hand-made from rare types of wood and cloth. There were many candles shining from the window sills. Edward felt amazed, this place was magnificent. His thought process was suddenly disturbed by a man, who approached him and said, "Welcome to the Eagle, Master Edward." Edward scrutinised this man: he was tall and well-built; the way he was dressed would probably be best described by the majority as metrosexual. His pale face contrasted with his black hair. He was smoking a cigar and Edward could bet that his nails were painted. "I'm Dane Donton, the owner of this establishment." They shook hands.

"Good evening." Thompson forced a smile. "This place is impressive."

"Thank you. Sit, please." Dane showed him a chair and Edward sat down. He glanced at the room they were in. There were many waiters, dressed entirely in black, standing near a wall. Each table in the room was occupied and everybody in the room was dressed as if they came straight from a photoshoot for Vogue. Edward looked at the suit he was wearing and realised that something, what he perceived to be elegant and posh, suddenly appeared to be entirely mediocre. He did not enjoy this feeling. Suddenly, Justin raised his voice and said, "Dane is a gifted story teller."

"Thank you…" Dane bowed.

Suddenly, a woman approached Dane and kissed him on the cheek. "Good evening, master." Then she turned towards Edward and they both became paralysed. It was Olga. "Oh, Edward…" she smiled and looked into Dane's eyes… "What are you doing here?"

"Justin invited me." Edward kissed her hand.

"Weren't you supposed to leave town with Leo?"

"Plans changed, but we won't be coming back to the house. No worries." She laughed.

Then Edward saw Leo enter and leave the building. Strange. Dane was finishing some kind of a story. "…and this is why I decided to invite you for this feast for your stomach and your eyes as well as your ears." He grinned and set his eyes on Edward. "Honey," he looked at Olga, "sit with us for a second." There were six places at the table.

She took a seat next to Dane, then set her eyes on Edward. "Edward, tell us something about yourself. Where do you work?" Olga said.

"I'm a freelance journalist."

"Fantastic. What are you interested in apart from writing?"

"I enjoy running. But I focus mostly on writing about cultural minorities as well as a cultural discrimination."

Olga cut in. "Dane, would you come with me for a second to the lobby?"

"Of course, my dear." He followed her towards the entrance.

A young man sitting next to Edward took a sip of wine, leaned towards Edward, and whispered, "Let me tell you a story, Edward. There was a woman, who came on vacation to a tropical island. She loved swimming in the ocean and spent the majority of her time on this favourite activity. The water was so salty, that sometimes it was enough for her to lie on her back and be carried by the water. She enjoyed sunbathing in this way. One day, a man joined her when she was sunbathing on it. He was a joyful person, so they became friends quickly and started spending the majority of their time together in the sea. The man was meeting the woman every day at the same time and they enjoyed their long discussions. He fell in love with this woman, therefore, one day, he took her to a lonely beach to impress her with the landscape. She fell in love with the view and they started visiting the beach on a daily basis to discuss this or that. They got on really well, but then came a day when the man took out an orange wooden box, when they were sunbathing on the beach, and handed it to the woman. She looked surprised, but opened the box eagerly. Then she became stone-faced. At the bottom of the box there was an inscription 'So do I'. The man took out a black pen and gave it to the woman. She could not comprehend the situation, so asked her friend to explain. He wanted her to write that she loves him on the other part of the box. The woman was apparently confused and replied: 'But I don't love you. I have a girlfriend.' He, filled with anger, looked at her and yelled 'So much time with you for nothing!' Then, he swam away and the woman has never seen him again. What do you think of this story, Edward?" The man leaned towards Thompson.

"I think that this guy was paranoid. Who would say 'I love you' in such a strange way? He must have been out of his mind." Edward stopped for a moment to observe his interlocutor's face. He seemed to be surprised. Justin, on the other hand, seemed confused.

The other, older man blinked a few times, took a sip of wine, and said, "My fault. Let me put this differently. What do you think about the woman's reaction?"

Edward did not enjoy this conversation. (Was this a joke or some anecdote?) "I think she was just honest. Spending time with somebody of the opposite sex does not mean that you are in love with them."

"She was a lesbian, Edward." Another man stared at him.

"I'm not following." Edward scratched his nose. "What was wrong about the woman then?"

"That she used him." The younger man's tone was harsh. "Look, he was sharing his love with her, showing her new places, keeping her good company. And she was simply playing with him."

Edward cleared his throat. "I do not agree. She was flawless. She treated him as a friend. Do you imply that she should have not engaged in this friendship, because she had a girlfriend? Can't we have friends? I do not see your point and think that the guy you portrayed in that story is repulsive. I'm on the girl's side."

The two men looked anxious, a few people were glancing at Edward from other tables. Justin spoke in a soothing voice. "I guess our starters are coming. Perfect." Dane came back and glanced at Edward. "Olga had to leave earlier. In the meantime, I also got an important call from my wife, so I need to leave immediately. Owen, Jade, come to my house in an hour. Justin, take Master Thompson for a drink or something." He looked at two men, who were sitting at a table with a bewildered Justin and more than confused Edward. Then he departed.

One of the men raised his voice. "Tell us something more about your work, Edward."

Edward had a foreboding that this was going to be a tough hour. His theory proved to be true as he was not willing to dwell on weird stories about homosexuals and their deeds, which resulted in a lack of themes to discuss. Thompson was trying to get to know some more about Olga and Leo's occupations, but their friends were rather erratic on that. Olga was supposed to be jobless, and Leo was a part of some kind of a hedge fund. Edward was not a specialist if it came to hedge funds, so they did not discuss that either. Justin was rather quiet during the whole evening and the two men, Jade and Owen, seemed to be strongly biased if it came to homosexuality. Personally, Edward had never cared much about other people's personal lives and could not comprehend the youngest man's willingness to elaborate on those topics. Why should they dwell on this and make it an issue? Wouldn't it be easier to concentrate on climate change, wars and health problems than on somebody's love life? Owen's approach seemed ridiculous and that is why Edward decided to leave the town as quickly as possible to free himself from uncomfortable discussions with not the right kind of people. Before leaving the Eagle, he asked Justin, "How did you get to know Olga?"

"I had never met that woman, frankly speaking."

"And Owen and Jade?"

"I met them twice and they seemed to be really cool guys. Today the conversation was a bit uncomfortable for me though. I'm sorry it turned out to be like this. The first two meetings were kind of different. I guess you didn't have a good time."

"Well," Ed sighed, "I felt as if those guys were interrogating me all the time. Where do you live? Do you have a wife? What are your views on this or that? How old are you? My friend, who was gay… blah blah blah. Jesus."

"That was my last meeting with this Dane. And I'm sorry for not telling you about the kind of clothing to wear. But I did not know it would be so posh in there. By the way, did you know Dane before?"

"No. Why?"

"Well, he knew your surname and I didn't tell him that."

When Edward returned to the Tiny House, he decided to pack everything and leave the very next morning, when, suddenly, Jonathan called. "Hi! My flight was cancelled, so I'm flying out tomorrow morning. I'm furious." He sounded exactly like that.

"That sucks."

"Eddie, how was your dinner?"

Edward sighed. "Terrible. How is that this Olga owns two houses if she is unemployed, Jon?"

"She is not unemployed, but on retirement, Eddie."

Silence. Edward was surprised. "How can she possibly be on retirement if she's younger than me? She's in her early thirties."

"Wait. What?! Who are you talking about?" Jonathan sounded alarmed.

"Jonathan, what does the owner look like?"

"She is in her seventies, quite chubby, but very elegant. She has long silver hair, which she wears in a bun, and yes, her name is Olga. She is an elderly person, Eddie. What does this woman you're talking about look like?"

"She is a thin blonde with short hair and, as I recall, blue eyes. Jonathan, what the hell is going on?" Edward felt uneasy and the room suddenly became too hot for him. "This woman told me that she owns the house. I am sure about this. She even told me that she needed to clean up a bit in it."

"You know what? I will call Olga and hope that she'll be able to explain this situation to me, all right?"

Ed sighed. "OK, I'll wait."

Jonathan hung up, leaving Edward alone with his thoughts. He started analysing the situation. Something was clearly wrong. He kept standing near the stairs and listening to make sure he was alone. He went upstairs, checked the bathroom, scrutinised the kitchen, the living room and the garage. There was nobody else in the house. Olga and Leo's suitcases were gone and the whole place looked marvelously clean. There were no traces of all the dirty snow they accidentally brought on their shoes into the house. Each bin was emptied. Suddenly, Edward recalled the kitchen conversation. Olga was doing something with plastic bags and tapes, and claimed that she needed to rearrange some things and clean up. OK, that made some sense. But she also said that this was what she did when at home, and this building did not belong to her. She was lying to him. Edward was also pretty sure that at night, when they woke him up, she referred to Leo as her "husband", not boyfriend. When they met in the morning, she told Edward that Leo was her boyfriend. Why was she pretending to be the owner? How did they get access to the house? Edward tried to calm down, yet, suddenly, he became paralysed by fear. How the heck did Dane Donton know his surname? When Ed met the couple, they got to know solely each other's names, not surnames. If the woman did not own the house, she could have not known anything about him coming over and therefore, she could have not known anything about him, including his surname. Yet, this bloody Dane referred to him by Ed's name and surname, so how the hell did he know? The phone rang, it was Jonathan again.

"Ed, I've spoken to Olga and she is very alarmed by this situation. She told me that nobody except her, me, and now you has access to the house. She doesn't know any young girl named Olga. The only young person she is in touch with is her cleaning lady, but she is Latino and in her twenties. She does not remember giving the keys to anybody."

"Fuck. So who are these people?"

"I don't know, Edward. Maybe some crazy young couple, who enjoys breaking into other people's houses?"

"They don't look as if they needed to break in anywhere, Jonathan. Look, I've seen them at the Eagle today and this couple clearly rubs shoulders with opulent people. The restaurant is super exclusive and everybody seems to be maniacal about expensive designs. Should we go with this to the police?"

Jonathan sighed. "What will we tell them? That an elderly lady does not remember if she gave the keys to her home to anybody except me and that you met at this house a young couple, whom you happened to bump into at a super-expensive restaurant? Yeah, they will for sure help us, we'll be on their priority list." Jonathan seemed grievous. "What actually do you know about them?"

"They made me believe that the woman's the owner. I am pretty sure that they're married, but had a reason to keep me misinformed. This 'Olga' was telling me about her aim to clean up the house, as she usually does that with her Tiny House. She had a lot of tapes and plastic bags in the kitchen. I have never told them my surname, but this Olga took Dane outside of the room, and, when he came back, he knew it. Justin swears Donton could have not possibly got to know it from him. So, Olga must have told him that. And, judging from the dinner conversation with their friends, they have some issues with accepting the fact that there are homosexual people living in this world. That's all I know. I have no photos of them. Do you know the Eagle restaurant?"

"I've never been there, but I know it exists. Do you know where they may be now?"

"I have no clue. Hey, what if your friend just cannot remember that this woman had the keys to her house? This is also a possibility."

"Well, she tends to forget certain things from time to time. Eddie, I think you should return here, and forget about the whole thing."

"I'm returning tomorrow morning. Sleep well, Jon."

"See you, buddy." Jonathan hung up.

Edward went upstairs, took a hot shower, and jumped into bed. He took his laptop from a suitcase and googled the restaurant he had just returned from to read the description of this posh place. The site was elegantly designed and showed beautiful photos of the interior. He clicked on the "contact" button and saw the photo of Dane Donton accompanied by a phrase *"What we value most is excellence"*. How ordinary was that. There were two emails on the site: the first was **theeagle@gmail.com**, and the second (for business purposes) **danedonton@gmail.com**. Then Edward caught a glimpse of the description of the restaurant and hotel's operation, which took him aback. It said that the Eagle was a place for organising events and conferences and implied that one cannot go there just like that and eat a dinner, because the establishment is used solely for business purposes and a variety of large-scale events. Peculiar. They entered the Eagle just like that, with the owner of course, but if the restaurant did not serve individual guests, then who were all of those elegant people? Edward had been to places which operate under similar conditions in order to interview the owners and write articles about them later, but if there was a party going on, the owners would always take him to their private room and the food would be served there as well. They would show him around, but never disturb a private event. This is not what happened with Dane Donton as they did not tell Edward that there was a party (or conference?) going on at the Eagle. Edward suddenly felt a desire to interview Dane and write an article about the Eagle, its history and development. The place was, with no doubt, spectacular, thus Donton should be eager to make Edward help him promote his luxurious hotel and restaurant. He decided to call him tomorrow, texted Jonathan that he would not be coming back yet, and went to sleep in the cosy twin bed, where even bedclothes were changed by Leo and Olga from the white ones to the beige and clean ones to make him feel comfortable again.

19th February 2015

Edward woke up at 7.00 a.m. as he tended to do. He slept well and not for long, as usual, so there was no need to stay in bed. He jumped out of it and headed downstairs. He got a message from Sally that she would be back at 8.00 p.m. on May 1st and that everything was going well. Edward fetched his laptop and went to the kitchen to prepare some coffee, which turned out to be the only eatable product present in there. He'd have to go shopping then, yet not eagerly as it began snowing heavily again. He booted his computer and created an email for Dane Donton:

From: edwardthompson@gmail.com
To: danedonton@gmail.com
Subject: Interview for a magazine
Dear Dane,
Thank you for yesterday's dinner. I am impressed by the quality of the service and appearance of the Eagle. As you already know, I am a journalist, and I

would be grateful if you would like to tell me more about your establishment, your history and future prospects so that we could create an article promoting the Eagle. I would be grateful if you managed to find some time for this interview.
Best regards,
Edward Thompson

He pressed the "send" button, got up and went to purchase some groceries.

Edward was back after two hours, as apart from shopping, he decided to save some time and eat a breakfast at Starbucks. Maybe that was a waste of money, but he relished their chai and cheese panini. Having entered the kitchen, he checked his email box and saw a message from Dane Donton. He was not expecting such a reply.

From: danedonton@gmail.com
To: edwardthompson@gmail.com
Subject: Re: Interview for a magazine
Dear Edward,
Unfortunately, I am busy right now and have no time for interviews. The Eagle's reputation is flawless

and we have many returning customers, therefore I see no point in publishing any articles about us.
Kind regards,
Dane Donton

Edward kept staring at the email with a feeling of deep disappointment. Probably Dane's clients were wealthy and valued anonymity. This explanation did not sound reasonable, but it was the only one Thompson could manage to come up with. Usually, that kind of entrepreneur enjoyed promoting their locals to gain even more customers and make more money. That is exactly the law of supply: the more people are willing and able to purchase your products or services in a given time period, the higher the prices may be and the greater profits you made. Maybe Dane did not care about money? This was of course unlikely as how else could he purchase more of his Gucci shoes and Armani suits? Maybe his bank account could be characterised by seven zeros? Edward could not possibly know the answer to that. He decided to call his sister, who went with James for their honeymoon in Sri Lanka. His sister answered the phone.

"Hello, Eddie!"

"Hi! How are you doing?"

"Oh! Couldn't be better! Today we tasted some red bananas and they were delicious. So small and red." Judging from her voice those bananas must have been really tasty.

"I've never ever eaten something like that. Were they red inside?"

"No, inside they were pale yellow. Listen, I can't reach Harry, I'm worried. Do you have any news?" Edward had completely forgotten about Harry Bellman's disappearance. "Uhh, I've been so busy lately that I have no clue. I will ask about that if you want me to."

"Could you do it? Thanks. At the beginning, we were pissed off, but now we're getting worried. He has always had some drinking issues, but, if needed, he could manage to be sober and attend any meeting. We now blocked the majority of calls as many people call us in the middle of the night, 'cause they either don't know that we are where we are or they are simply unaware of the time difference. Ugh."

"OK, get it. I'll figure out what is going on with Harry and call you back. Who may be best informed?"

"Uncle Fred knew him particularly well, so you should call him."

"No problem. I'll call you back."

Edward hung up and chose Frank's number.

"Eddie! My favourite nephew!"

"Hi!" Edward could not help but smile at the sound of Frank's friendly voice.

"What's up?"

"Have you found Harry?"

Pause. "No, we did not. We went to the police with that, but I don't think they will be serious about him being missing, 'cause he's been disappearing quite often recently. I think he has a friend, if you know what I mean…" Frank giggled. "You don't know Harry well, but he is like that. The only exception here is that he has always been loyal to his friends, and it's highly improbable that he would dare to let down his close buddies. However, something like that could take place if he was head over heels… you know. That is Harry."

"OK. Thanks, Frank. Let me know if he reappears."

"If you have some time, come over and visit me. You're always welcome."

"I'll let you know when. See you."

"Bye, Eddie!"

Edward unpacked all the groceries and made himself some green tea. Damn, they really cleaned up the house... Everything was so polished and shining. Amazing. He started pacing up and down the living room and gazed at the brown couch. He wondered what was actually wrong with it. It did not seem to be broken. It looked rather elegant and comfortable. He walked around the couch and, eventually, sat on it while still sipping his green tea. Then he felt a smell. He has never felt such a smell before, but it could be best described as a smell of decaying meat. He stood up and gazed at the couch again. What was wrong with it? He put his mug on a coffee table and set his eyes on the brown piece of furniture. Then, he started reassembling it to see if it could be transformed into a bed. The process went swiftly and now the couch consisted of three adjacent parts. The one situated in the middle was a kind of a box, where one can put all the duvets and pillows. The nauseating smell became stronger. Edward felt instantly sick when he saw the box: there were blood stains on it. Being a journalist, he took out his iPhone and took a picture of the couch. Then, he opened the box and vomited. Before touching anything, he took a photo of the interior. Harry Bellman's body looked as if it was in a bathtub filled with blood. His facial expression could be best described by one short word: fear. The interior of the box was strengthened by plastic bags and tape so that the blood was prevented from leaking outside. He called the police.

20th February 2015

Edward was brought in for interrogation and forbidden to leave the town as solely his fingerprints could be found in the Tiny House, which made him the main suspect, at least for the moment. Now it made sense why the couple cleaned everything up so well. Uncle Frank promised to prepare him a room to sleep at his house in the suburbs. Edward did not mourn much after Harry as he had seen him barely once, but Uncle Frank was deeply shattered. The body was placed at the Tiny House on the 16th of February around 1.00 a.m., so an hour before the couple woke Edward up. This would explain their behavior and lack of word awareness. Frank had never seen a corpse like that and he felt pain when he thought about the condition of the body: Harry had been stabbed multiple times and his genitals were cut away. Police claimed that there existed a strong probability that Harry was brought alive to the Tiny House, yet his mouth was sealed with tape. His arms and legs were strongly tied, Olga and Leo put him in the box in the couch and subsequently, they slashed him and left him for Edward to find. He was trying to figure out what happened, when Uncle Frank stood up and involuntarily bumped his left wrist against Edward's right shoulder.

"Sorry," he said quietly and went to fetch some tissues. He could not stop sniffling.

This made Edward think of something. Something, which made no sense. Or maybe it DID?

"Frank? Could you come in here?"

"Coming." Uncle slowly joined Edward on a sofa.

"Can you bump into me in the same way you have just done?"

"OK." Frank was uninterested in Edward's experiment. The only thing he was thinking of at the moment was Harry and his unjust fate.

When Frank fulfilled Ed's request, Edward's eyes started shining. "That could not have been a watch scratch." He articulated each word carefully.

"What?" Frank seemed to be absent-minded.

"Frank!" Edward shook him by the shoulders and looked him deep in the eyes. "This guy, Leo, he must have given me a dose of a sleeping drug."

"What do you mean?" Frank seemed helpless.

"He accompanied me to the garage and brought in a blanket and some pillows. I felt sudden pain, but he excused himself for 'scratching me with his watch'. But that could not have been a watch." He articulated each syllable with utmost care. "I t w a s a s y r i n g e. He must have given me a sleeping drug. This makes perfect sense. I was exhausted and not really aware of the situation. My top priority was to get a full night's sleep. I could not see his left hand when he was handing all of that stuff to me, I didn't pay much attention either. He told me that it was a watch and I accepted this explanation. I didn't give a damn. I fell asleep immediately and never really checked my arm. I was wearing long and tight-fitting sleeves. Look, this must have been a quite a dose, because I usually sleep for a maximum seven hours, not twelve. I am going to go to perform a toxicologist examination and maybe they will confirm my suspicions. That may not help at all, but I will talk to the cops."

23rd February 2015

The examination could not back up Edward's theory as too many days had passed from the supposed injection. The doctor told him that in case of such injections it was impossible to find any trace of the drug in the blood after twenty-four hours and there would usually remain no visible spot of where the needle pricked one's skin, unless somebody was allergic to such a substance (which was rare). Logically thinking, Leo and Olga used their opportunity well: they removed their fingerprints from the inside of the house and left the body with Edward. Were they trying to frame him? Probably yes. Would they succeed? Hopefully not. First, Edward did not know Harry Bellman. Second, they could check his mobile conversations with Jonathan to understand Edward's predicament. Third... what was that? Edward went to see what Uncle Frank was doing and saw him reading a book.

"Why would somebody do this to Harry, Frank? You knew him very well. What could be the motive?" Edward sat down on a chair close to Frank.

"I don't know." He sighed heavily. "Harry had some drinking issues, but overall, he was a good man. He had never had any issues with other people. He was spectacular at his job as a dance choreographer. I don't see any reason why somebody would like to harm him like this."

"You said he had a girlfriend, right?"

Frank cleared his throat. "He had girlfriends long ago... He used to have boyfriends, Eddie. Harry was a homosexual, I thought you knew that."

Edward felt a sudden anxiety. "What do you know about the Eagle, Frankie?"

"This is a hotel and a restaurant. Top-notch and that kind of stuff."

"And Dane Donton?"

"I don't know him."

"He's the owner. Look, Justin took me to dinner with him, and the guys who were dining with us seemed to be obsessed with homosexuality. From what I could understand, they would like to eradicate it and think of it as of some bloody form of evil. And that was literally all they could talk about. Homo, homo, homo... Fuck me. It was as if they were trying to indoctrinate me or something... Indoctrinate and interrogate. Anyways, when I got back home I looked through all web info about the Eagle and found out that it's a place used solely for conferences and large-scale parties. Therefore, my question is: why would they dine with me in the middle of somebody's party? This Dane was super-elegant. Everybody looked similar. People from other tables were glancing at me furtively from time to time and I thought that they were doing this due to my not-Armani-suit. Listen, Frank. Maybe they belong to some kind of a secret society or something? When I wrote to Dane to ask him for an interview, he replied that the Eagle did not need any additional advertisements. This is not how folks usually react."

"But what is the connection between this potential society and Harry?"

"I am convinced that Olga and Leo murdered Harry. Maybe, because he was a homosexual?"

"Is there any way you could prove this theory to be true?"

Suddenly, Edward's phone rang. "Hey, Jonathan."

"I've spoken to Olga. And this 'Olga' of yours must have been the previous cleaning lady of my friend. She fits the description perfectly. We're sure that this woman introduced herself as Olga, 'cause she realised that real Olga knows about your stay at Tiny House. That makes perfect sense. But, Leo is a real name of her husband. They didn't change it as they must have known you might have remembered his name during that night. She tried to assure you that she has no husband, 'cause she should have forgotten that they used the 'husband' word that night. Listen, Eddie, this woman's real name is Martha Kline. I've just talked to the police about this and they will search her house. I'll be in touch with you."

"Damn. Makes sense. I'm pretty sure that they drugged me to make me sleep soundly and not disturb them while dealing with the body and cleaning up."

"Seriously?"

"Yes, I cannot prove it but I am convinced I am right."

"Damn. Do you have any suspicions why Harry was murdered and mutilated like that?"

"I've just talked to Frank about this and got to know that he was a homosexual."

"Somebody killed him, 'cause he was gay? Jesus…"

"When I went to dinner with Justin, I saw Olga, sorry, Martha and Leo there. Martha left very quickly as if my presence was disturbing her. The two other men Justin and I were dining with seemed to be obsessed about homosexuality and gave me the impression that they despised such people. To cut the long short: I am pretty sure there exists some kind of a dumb crazy organisation, probably with its headquarters at the Eagle, which gets rid of not straight people. Justin doesn't know it well, 'cause it was his third meeting with Dane, so he has little knowledge about what Dane exactly does. I also know that Justin has never heard again from Dane after bringing me to the Eagle."

"But, man, this makes no sense. The question you should ask is: what did they gain from this murder? And how did they get to know that he was gay?"

"Satisfaction? Maybe they are mental or something. Mental people very often pretend to be kind and friendly. I'm going to see the police and tell them that it would be wise to search for proof that Martha and Leo did belong to some kind of an organisation linked to Donton, thus the Eagle. Those two people are smart badasses though, so I guess that home search won't help us much."

"Call me if you have some news."

25th February 2015

The search of Martha's apartment turned out to be futile as predicted. There was also no trace of either her, or Leo as if they had evaporated into thin air. Harry's funeral was planned for the next day and Edward could not stop thinking over again and again and again the whole situation. He was pissed off, because it all seemed so simple, yet so complex. What bloody motive could this damned couple have to eliminate Harry? And was Dane involved? Ed decided to conduce his very own investigation and started by searching for any similar killings on the web. He found one relatively recent article about a homosexual, who was beaten to death in December 2014, but the murderer had already been placed behind the bars. He could not find any similar cases and felt deeply disappointed. If this organisation's (if it exists of course) goal was not to search for fulfilment and satisfaction steaming from taking away lives of the homosexuals, then what was it? He needed to find out and the best method would be to talk to Dane.

Edward reached the Eagle in forty minutes and entered the building. He asked the receptionist whether Dane Donton was present, which he was. He headed towards his office, knocked, and entered with no permission. Dane stood up in surprise. "What the hell are you doing here?!"

"Hello, Dane, why are you greeting me in this way?" Edward sat down.

Dane sat down as well, lit a cigar and looked at Ed in utter fury. "I invited you for a dinner and told you that I did not want any interviews. And then what happens? You spread some fucking rumours about me murdering homosexuals. This is insane and purely stupid. Because of you, the police are ruining my reputation by questioning my employees and guests. *Quel horreur!*" he added in French.

"I was solely answering their questions. I have no real insight into the case, Dane. I will leave if you answer my query though: why did we sit at a table in a room, where there was a party going on?"

"What do you mean?" Dane squinted his eyes.

"You organise only parties and conferences. Individuals cannot dine here. So why were we eating in a room, when there was a party going on?"

"Because that was my party, organised for my closest friends, and it was my decision to let you in. Good bye, Mr. Thompson. You should leave now. I'm busy."

"How did you get to know my surname?"

"Martha told me you surname."

"What Martha?"

Dane started sweating. "Olga, sorry, her second name is Martha."

"That's interesting, because I have never told her what my surname is."

Dane stood up abruptly and said through his teeth, "G e t t h e h e l l o u t."

"Good bye, Donton." Edward stood up and took a furtive glance at Dane's wall of honour. He managed to spot a photo of a large group of people when he was leaving the room. He wished he had recorded this conversation.

24th June 2015

The case remained unresolved as the police could not find any strong evidence to confirm Edward's theory. There was no proof of Dane Donton's involvement, neither of Martha's or Leo's. No fingerprints, literally noth-

ing. Do you want to know the truth about the murder of Harry Bellman? Let me tell you then. There did exist a secret society launched by Donton's father. Yes, Edward was right about EVERYTHING. The police omitted one important question – how did Donton really make his money? Because it did not come from organising parties. The Eagle was just a cover-up for devilish operations of a bunch of crafty individuals, who shared one trait – hatred towards homosexuals. The Eagle did organise a party from time to time to convince everybody that it was a regular restaurant and hotel, yet Donton did not need this money and was not interested in such a form of entrepreneurship. That is exactly why he was not willing to give interviews and did not need advertisement. And the reason why he did not need it lay in the fact that he had steady inflows of cash from Yemen, Iran, Iraq, Mauritania, Nigeria, Qatar, Saudi Arabia, Somalia, Sudan and United Arab Emirates. Why those countries? Cannot you see a linking point? In all of the above-mentioned states homosexuality may be punished by death. Yet, in all of those countries homosexuality does exist among each social group. We are afraid of death. The more money we have, the more afraid we may be of losing it all. And that is precisely the reason why Dane's society kept on spying on and blackmailing homosexuals inhabiting those countries. The organisation kept on bringing in the money. If you think that it would be easy to uncover the truth, you are mistaken. Dozens of people were involved in the organisation's undercover operations. And those people shared another trait –opulence, hence access to a variety of resources others would not be able to afford. What tended to happen if any blackmail victim did not comply? Simple, they would be eliminated and somebody would be framed for the murder. Each murder differed, so linking the dots was impossible. Who was Harry? Harry used to be a part of the organisation, but then, one day, he realised he fancied men more than women. The organisation knew Harry wanted to leave. Martha and Leo were a part of the organisation and executed Bellman for treachery, thus the mutilation – a warning to others. They tried to frame Edward, but forgot that he did not really know the victim. That is why their plan did not fully work. However, nobody will ever be jailed for the crime as the police will never find enough proof. The photos taken by Edward will not be considered valuable. Edward Thompson will remain the main suspect, and basically the only one as Leo and Martha disappeared as quickly as they appeared at the Tiny House during this night in February. Edward will gain the reputation of an individual who should not be trusted due to being a murder suspect. His wife, his uncle, and his sister will remain uncertain about what really happened. The majority of us will never get to know the truth, yet will be satisfied with the presumption that some "Edward Thompson" deprived Harry Bellman of his life. But has history proven that a regular man's word against the words of the resourceful ones tends to be decisive?

-END-

I WOULD LIKE TO THANK…

… my mother, father, and younger brother, who impressed me with their patience and willingness to listen to my crazy ideas. I love you so much and I am so grateful for my mother's precious piece of advice while trying to make my stories both realistic and accurate!